Molly Maguire:

WIDE
RECEIVER

ANN SULLIVAN lives in Colorado with her husband, their eight children, and an Old English sheepdog named Wilbur. The idea for this book came to her as she watched a girl from her son's class walking to practice one day, hair streaming down her back, helmet swinging from her arm, and a big wad of gum in her mouth.

Molly Maguire:

WIDE RECEIVER

ANN SULLIVAN

AN AVON  CAMELOT BOOK

MOLLY MAGUIRE: WIDE RECEIVER is an original publication of Avon Books. This work has never before appeared in book form.

AVON BOOKS
A division of
The Hearst Corporation
1350 Avenue of the Americas
New York, New York 10019

Copyright © 1992 by Ann Sullivan
Published by arrangement with the author
Library of Congress Catalog Card Number: 91-92465
ISBN: 0-380-76114-9
RL: 4.7

First Avon Camelot Printing: August 1992

CAMELOT TRADEMARK REG. U.S. PAT. OFF. AND IN OTHER COUNTRIES, MARCA REGISTRADA, HECHO EN U.S.A.

Printed in the U.S.A.

OPM 10 9 8 7 6 5 4 3 2 1

To Bill—
my husband, my friend,
my computer operator

Chapter One

"Hurry, Arabella. We're going to be late," Molly said, breaking into a half run.

"I'm hurrying as fast as I can. My legs aren't as long as yours, you know," her best friend Arabella complained, shifting her books to her other arm and trying hard to keep up with Molly. But Molly had the fastest legs in the whole fifth grade, so that wasn't easy.

They charged up the steps of Lincoln Elementary and scooted into their seats just as the bell rang.

Molly sat down and put her books away while Miss Bloom took roll. Jason Jenson sat right behind Molly. His fingers began poking in her back. He started singing that awful song under his breath, "RED HAIR, RED HAIR, IS THAT THE COLOR OF YOUR UNDERWEAR?"

1

Molly felt her face burn. If only she could punch Jason's lights out! Someday . . .

"Molly."

Miss Bloom was calling on her.

"Molly? Do you have your science homework?" she asked patiently for the second time.

"Yes, Ma'am. I have it right here," Molly answered, leaning sideways to pull her Pee Chee folder out from the storage area in her desk.

She opened the Pee Chee and felt her stomach drop.

"It was here when I came to school. Honest," Molly said, diving back into her desk to see if the paper had somehow gotten stuck with her books.

It hadn't. Her homework assignment was gone.

Molly looked up at Miss Bloom. "I did it. I swear I did it. And I brought it to school. Honest. I don't know what could have happened to it."

Miss Bloom didn't look happy. "You will spend your lunch time in here doing your science homework. Jason? Do you have yours?"

"Yes, Miss Bloom. Right here," he answered, holding up his paper.

As Miss Bloom went up and down the rows asking for homework, Jason whispered, "That's okay, Flame. Girls don't need science anyway."

"Don't be dumb, Jason. *Everyone* needs science. And don't call me *Flame.*"

"Not girls. My dad says all girls need to know is how to cook and clean house. You don't need science for that, Flame."

Molly felt her temper rising, but she clamped her mouth shut. Miss Bloom was looking at her

2

and she was already in trouble. It wouldn't be worth getting in more trouble by talking to that idiot.

At recess the boys were throwing a football around, and Molly and Arabella stood by watching.

"Wish we could play," muttered Molly.

"Let's go play dodgeball with the other girls."

"I want to play football."

"Why?"

"I *love* football. It's the most fun thing to do in the whole world," Molly said, watching the ball arc through the air from Jason to Ray. Ray pulled his arm back and threw the ball to Bobby, but Bobby wasn't paying attention. The ball came right toward Molly and she caught it with ease.

For a split second she thought of running with it, racing like the wind. She knew the boys would never catch up with her, and it would feel wonderful to beat them at their own game.

But in the next minute, the bell rang and recess was over.

"Throw it here," Jason said, commanding Molly to give up the ball.

Reluctantly, she did.

As they got in line, Jason said, "How's your . . . red hair?"

"Just fine, thank you. And so's my underwear."

"Find your homework yet?" he asked, laughing wickedly.

It came to Molly like a flash. "You took it, didn't you," she said.

3

"Prove it," Jason said.

Molly was burning. Of course she couldn't prove it. He had probably thrown it away already.

Mad as she was, her ears perked up when she heard Jason and Ray talking.

"Don't forget, sign ups for Parks and Recreation football is tomorrow."

"Yeah. Even Bobby's going to play this year. I can't wait."

Parks and Recreation football. I wonder . . . , Molly thought, following the boys into school.

Molly's next door neighbor, Mr. Brewer, was raking leaves in his front yard when she got home from school. He put down his rake and called to her.

"Got a few minutes for an old man, Girl?"

Molly laughed. Mr. Brewer was her all-time favorite person. He had been the Maguires' neighbor for as long as she could remember. His wife had died a few years ago, and Molly knew he was lonely. Besides, they had something in common that kept them close. Mr. Brewer loved football, too.

"I 'spose you want me to rake leaves," Molly sighed, bending to pick up the rake.

"No, I don't. You know me better than that, Girl," Mr. Brewer protested, taking the rake from her. "I feel like tossing the old pigskin around. I need someone to catch it."

Molly grinned and went over to the planter Mrs. Brewer used to have filled with geraniums.

Since her death, the flowers had been replaced by Mr. Brewer's football and pieces of rope and old newspapers. Molly picked up the football and tossed it to Mr. Brewer, then got in position to catch his pass.

The ball came at her like a bullet. Molly stepped forward and met it eagerly, satisfied with the slap of palms against leather. She kept her fingers supple and spread wide, molding them to the ball.

"Girl, you're a natural," Mr. Brewer said admiringly. "Your hands stick to that ball like flypaper."

He drew his arm back and threw the football to Molly's left, out of her reach. She ran hard, keeping her eyes on the ball, and caught it against her chest.

"Good catch! Too bad you weren't around forty years ago. Frank Leahy could have used you."

"Who's Frank Leahy?"

"He was my coach at Notre Dame," Mr. Brewer said, firing another pass. "He was as tough on us as a hammer on nails, but we learned to play the game."

"Wish I could play the game," Molly said sadly.

"By the time you're old enough for college, girls will be playing football at Notre Dame. You mark my words," Mr. Brewer said, lobbing the ball across the yard.

"College is a million years away. I mean now, this year. I wish I could play football on a real team *now*."

"If you keep practicing like this, you'll be a

5

shoo-in when you get to junior high. You're already better than most boys your age."

"Yeah, but that doesn't get me on a team," Molly muttered to herself.

She raced around the yard, catching hard to reach passes and trying to fake out Mr. Brewer by running with the ball in unexpected zigzag patterns.

She pretended Mr. Brewer was Jason and she was playing against him in an all-star game. In her imagination, she whizzed right by Jason and made a touchdown while he stood there with his mouth hanging open.

Too bad it wasn't for real.

She knew she could play football every bit as well as Jason, maybe better.

The idea that had started forming in her head at recess began to take shape.

Why not? she thought. *It would serve him right.*

As soon as she went inside, she called Arabella and explained her plan.

"You're crazy. There's no way you can get away with it."

"Yes there is. I'll get my sister to help me."

"I don't understand you, Molly. Whenever I ask you to go to the mall or watch videos with me, you always say you're too busy building forts or floating rafts on the lake or climbing trees. Now this. Why can't you like clothes and rock stars and stuff instead of being such a tomboy?"

"I do like those things, Arabella. Only I like other stuff, too. I'll go to the mall with you next weekend. Promise."

6

"Sure you will." Arabella's voice was flat.

When Molly hung up the phone, she thought about how different she and Arabella were. Arabella liked wearing dresses and fixing her hair and reading silly fan magazines. Molly mostly liked to wear jeans, and she loved to be outside running or climbing or just *doing*. Her hair was a nuisance and she didn't really like fixing it and trying new hair styles.

But, she thought, *Arabella's right. I've got to start doing more girl things. One of these days. Maybe after I play football . . .*

7

Chapter Two

Molly draped her skinny legs over the end of the bed. She hoped her big sister Colleen had forgotten she was there. Colleen could get nasty and yell at Molly for watching her put on makeup or fix her hair.

"Why are you always watching me?" she'd yell.

And Molly would think, *because you're so pretty and when I get to be sixteen, I want to look just like you.* But Molly never said that out loud. She usually said something that made Colleen mad, like, "I've always been interested in clowns." Colleen threw shoes at Molly, but Molly usually got away before the shoes hit.

That's how it usually went. But today, Molly was practically holding her breath so Colleen wouldn't notice her. She didn't want to upset Colleen today.

"Colleen, why don't you wear lipstick?"

"Don't you know anything? *No one* wears lipstick."

"Mom does."

"You're so dumb. Mom's forty. No one under forty wears lipstick. All the high school girls wear lip gloss or Vaseline."

Colleen looked at Molly through the mirror. "Someday, even *you* may grow up. But when you do, don't wear lipstick. It's *disgusting*." She went back to dabbing something white under her eyes.

Molly hesitated, unsure whether Colleen was in the proper frame of mind to hear her plan. Then she blurted it all out, deciding to take her chances.

"Well, what do you think? Will you do it for me?"

"I think you're dealing from half a deck. What did Mom say?"

"I didn't tell her. I know she wouldn't let me. Please, Colleen? I'll do something for you someday."

"What do I have to do?"

"Just take my lawn mowing money for the registration fee, fill out the application, and bring home the uniform."

"For Pete's sake. My sister, the jock."

"Oh thanks, Colleen! Don't forget to sign my name as 'Lee.' They don't have to know it's short for Molly."

"I don't know when I can get the uniform home. I have to be at school an hour early tomorrow, then I have play rehearsal after school. Mom

9

and Dad have to go with me for a conference in the morning, so I can't do it then."

"They do?" Molly's eyes took on a gleam Colleen didn't notice. "That's okay. Thanks, Colleen. I really appreciate it."

Molly went to bed with a secret smile on her face. She couldn't wait! She was going to play football with the boys, only they wouldn't know it was she. And she was going to be the best darned player on the team. Then, and only then, would she let Jason know it was she all along. And would he be mad!

As soon as everyone left the next morning, Molly started to work. She'd show Arabella that she wasn't so strange. She sat in front of Colleen's mirror and lathered makeup base all over her face, nice and thick. Amazing! Her jillions of freckles almost disappeared. Next she applied eye liner. It was kind of hard to stay close to her eyes, but the pencil didn't get too far off the track.

The blush brush—oh, that was neat. She brushed it all over her cheeks. Now they were good and rosy.

The mascara was going to be a problem. That took practice. Well, she had about five minutes—that should be enough practice.

She opened her eyes real wide like Colleen did, then started brushing mascara onto her eyelashes. She did quite well at first, then her hand slipped and she got mascara above her eye. She tried to wipe it off with her finger, but that just

10

smudged it. Oh well, it didn't look too bad. She smeared a gob of Vaseline on her mouth, then Molly stared at herself in the mirror. She looked so different! So grown up. Even Jason would think she looked nice, red hair or not. And Arabella couldn't accuse her of being a tomboy.

When Molly met Arabella at the corner, she smiled smugly. The fact that Arabella's mouth wouldn't close didn't bother Molly. She knew Arabella probably was wishing she had a big sister with lots of makeup, too.

"Well, what do you think?"

"You look different."

"I know. Neat, isn't it? And it's so easy to do."

"Mmmmmmm."

"Next time Colleen goes out for the evening, I'll have you over and we'll practice on you."

"Thanks, I think," muttered Arabella.

Molly continued to smile. Her teeth felt a little funny with Vaseline all over them, but she knew she looked terrific. She couldn't wait for Jason to see her.

She got to her seat before Jason arrived and watched Miss Bloom writing on the board. It wasn't long before she felt those fingers jabbing her in the back. Slowly, Molly turned around in her seat, lowering her eyelashes the way she'd seen Colleen do.

"Good grief!" screamed Jason. "Molly's bleeding all over her face!"

Miss Bloom rushed to Molly's desk, fear etched on her face. When Molly looked up, the fear was

11

replaced by shock. Then it was obvious Miss Bloom was trying hard not to laugh.

Molly was dismayed. *What's wrong with everybody? They're all laughing—at me.*

"Arabella, please take Molly to the lavatory and help her wash her face," Miss Bloom said. "Class, face front. Open your math books to page seventy-six."

Molly walked to the bathroom as if in a trance. Arabella was muttering something about how *she* thought Molly looked really nice, but Molly barely heard. She had never been so humiliated in her whole life.

Looking in the mirror above the sink, Molly tried to see what everyone was laughing at. She still thought the makeup looked nice, but maybe it was too much for daytime.

She accepted the wet paper towels Arabella handed her and began to scrub. She scrubbed and scrubbed. And scrubbed. And scrubbed some more. Some of that stuff just wouldn't come off.

"Want me to ask the janitor for some Ajax?" suggested Arabella.

"No. Just squirt some more of that soap on a paper towel for me. I'll get it off if I have to skin myself," Molly answered between clenched teeth.

She finally got rid of most of the makeup. Her face felt like she had used sandpaper on it and there were still black rings around her eyes, but it was the best she could do.

"Ready?" asked Arabella.

"I guess. Only . . ."

"Only what?"

12

"I don't want to go back in there."

"Aw, come on, Molly. Nobody's going to say anything."

"Wanna bet?"

"Miss Bloom won't let anyone make fun of you. You know that."

"I just feel so *stupid*."

"You've got more guts than anyone else in our class, so don't feel stupid. Come on, let's go. She'll send someone after us if we don't hurry."

Molly followed reluctantly. It took every ounce of courage she had to walk back into the fifth-grade classroom. She looked at the floor until she reached her desk, then she looked at her hands.

Miss Bloom continued working math problems on the board and asking the class to direct her, but Molly was sure everybody was looking at her. For some reason, Jason wasn't poking her as usual. He was probably holding both hands over his mouth so he wouldn't laugh out loud.

When the recess bell finally rang, Molly felt she could let out her breath. As the kids were filing out, Miss Bloom said, "Molly, I'd like to speak with you for a minute."

Arabella shot her a sympathetic glance, then everyone else was gone. It was just Molly and Miss Bloom.

Unexpectedly, Miss Bloom put her arm around Molly. She gave her a little squeeze and said, "I know you feel bad. I'm really sorry we all reacted that way. It was just such a surprise to see you with all that makeup on. Molly," Miss Bloom

13

held her at arm's length so she could look in her eyes. "I have something I want to give you. When you feel like being very grown up, you can use some. No one will see it, but it will make you feel . . . you know, like an adult."

Miss Bloom opened her bottom drawer and picked up a tiny gold bottle. She unscrewed the cap and sniffed, then held it out for Molly to smell. It was wonderful!

"Just a tiny bit, Molly. If you put too much on, it won't smell good. Just use a dab." She hugged her again, then said, "This is our secret. Something just between us ladies."

They both laughed, and Molly realized she didn't feel so terrible anymore.

She ran out to recess and joined Arabella with some other girls who were jumping rope.

"What'd she say?" Arabella's eyes were as big as saucers. "Did you get in trouble? Is she going to call your mom?"

"No, I didn't get in trouble and she's not going to call my mom. We just talked," Molly smiled, "like grownups."

"No kidding." Arabella closed her eyes and sighed. "I was holding my breath the whole time. I'm glad she didn't get mad."

Molly decided not to tell anyone, even Arabella, about the perfume. Somehow it wouldn't be so special if anyone else knew.

"Come on, Molly. You're next," the girls turning each end of the long rope called.

Molly jumped in as all the girls chanted,

"Cinderella, dressed in yellow
Went upstairs to kiss a fellow.
On the way she bit a snake.
How many doctors did it take?
One. . .Two. . .Three. . .Four. . .Five. . .Six. . ."

With each number the rope went faster until Molly tripped and stopped it. She was laughing and out of breath, then noticed Jason and his buddies watching her.

"Look guys, the raccoon can jump rope." They laughed and laughed.

Raccoon? Oh yes. The eyeliner around her eyes. Of course. Molly did a slow burn. She'd get that Jason if it was the last thing she ever did.

Chapter Three

Molly sat at the kitchen table with her books scattered all over. She had homework in every subject and didn't know where to begin.

Better start with science, she thought. *Get the worst over with first.*

When she opened her book, one of the pages toward the back felt lumpy. She opened it to that page and found a piece of paper folded up very small. She unfolded the paper and read the note scrawled across the top. *Oops! Look what I found. J.*

It was her missing science homework. He *did* take it. The creep!

She tackled her homework with a vengeance, pushing the pencil so hard on the paper it broke. She wished it were Jason and punched holes all through the paper.

When her mom came in, the kitchen table looked like a battlefield for World War Three, with broken pencils and pages of notebook paper filled with holes all over.

"What are you doing?" she asked with concern.

"Sorry, Mom. I'm just so mad at that stupid Jason Jenson I got carried away."

"Never mind him, dear. I made cookies today. Why don't you take some over to Mr. Brewer?"

"All right. I'm sure not getting anything else done."

Molly balanced the plate in one hand while she pushed the screen door open with the other.

She cut through the hedge and went up the porch to their neighbor's back door.

"Mr. Brewer," Molly yelled. "Can I come in?"

"Door's open," he called.

She heard him shuffling through the kitchen before she saw him.

"Ah," he said, looking at the cookies. "I think I just died and went to heaven."

Molly laughed.

"Shall we have tea or milk?" he asked.

"I'd like tea, but you can have milk if you want," Molly answered.

"Tea it is," he said, filling the kettle with water and turning on the stove.

When they were settled at the table with steaming cups of hot, spiced tea in front of them, Molly told Mr. Brewer about Jason stealing her homework and getting her in trouble.

"Honestly, he's such a dweeb."

"Dweeb?"

"You know. A jerk. Thinks he's God's gift to the world. He thinks only *boys* can do things."

"Oh, I see," nodded Mr. Brewer.

"I'm going to show him. I have a plan and when I'm finished, Jason Jenson won't know what hit him."

"Did something else happen today? Did that boy do something else to get you all fired up like this?"

"Not really. I mean, it wasn't him," she said, looking at her hands in her lap. Mr. Brewer's eyebrows went up, but he didn't say anything.

"I used some of Colleen's makeup and fixed myself up," she continued. "But it was wasted on those dumb fifth graders. They don't know class when it's staring them in the face."

"I'll bet you looked wonderful," Mr. Brewer said, smiling.

"I did. But don't tell Colleen. She'll skin me alive if she finds out I got into her makeup."

"It'll be our secret."

Funny. That was the second time that day an adult had offered to share a secret with her.

She almost told Mr. Brewer her *big* secret, then thought better of it. She wasn't taking any chances on her parents' finding out before she even had a chance to try. She'd tell them about it tonight. Maybe.

It sure was hard to keep such an important secret. She felt as though she was going to explode with excitement. If she didn't tell someone soon, it was going to pop right out by itself.

"Mr. Brewer?" Molly swallowed hard, losing her resolve.

"Yup?"

"Can I ask you something about football? Can you keep your helmet and face guard on all the time?"

"Now why would anyone want to do that?"

"Can you?"

"Well," Mr. Brewer looked thoughtful, then a terrific gleam shone in his eyes.

"Does this have anything to do with Colleen going into your house a minute ago with shoulder pads and all kinds of football equipment?"

"You mean she's home now? She's got the stuff?"

Mr. Brewer hooted and laughed and slapped his knee.

"Girl, you're a real crackerjack! You're going to get on the football team, aren't you?" He slapped his knee again, laughing like a loon.

"Practice starts pretty soon. I gotta go get ready," Molly said.

"You're going to need some help. Why don't you get your gear and bring it over? It'd tickle me purple to help you pull this off. Yesiree, you've got spunk."

Molly was glad to have Mr. Brewer in on her secret.

Chapter Four

Molly grabbed her football gear and brought it back to Mr. Brewer's house.

"Here it is," she said, laying the impressive pile at his feet. Her eyes were shiny as she surveyed her treasure.

"What goes on first?"

Mr. Brewer rubbed his chin thoughtfully. "Hand me those pants there," he pointed, then picked up some pads and tucked them inside the pants in neat little pockets made for them.

Holding up the pants, Molly saw how they looked like huge muscles above the knees. She couldn't wait to try them on.

"Now you hold still while I put this over your head," Mr. Brewer commanded, holding out the huge shoulder pads. They felt awfully funny clacking over her head, then resting like big turtles on her shoulders. Mr. Brewer pulled the laces tight and tied them, then helped Molly put on the gigantic jersey.

When she'd first seen the jersey she'd thought it was big enough to fit her dad, but now she realized it had to be big to go over those turtles.

"Go in the bathroom and put on these pants now," Mr. Brewer directed.

Molly looked at herself in the bathroom mirror. She recognized the long red hair and the face with the jillions of freckles, but nothing else. The girl in the mirror had gargantuan shoulders and bulging thighs. If Colleen could see her, Molly knew she would call her 'thunder thighs'.

She was pleased to see Mr. Brewer's face light up when she came out.

"How do I look?"

"Except for that red mane of yours, you look just like one of the guys," he grinned.

"I've got to do something about my hair." Molly pushed it up on top of her head and tried to put the helmet over it, but there were too many strands falling down.

"You're going to need a cap to hold it up," Mr. Brewer said, slowly shuffling off to his bedroom.

He came back with a white cotton cap.

"My wife wore this in the hospital. It's clean and it'll hold your hair up," he said, matter-of-factly.

Together they stuffed Molly's hair into the cap. It held. There was no telltale red showing now.

"One more thing," Mr. Brewer said, opening a kitchen drawer. He pulled something out and said, "These are safety goggles. They'll help to disguise your face, but you'll still be able to see. Try them on."

They were a little uncomfortable, but Molly knew she'd get used to them.

"Ready?" Mr. Brewer asked.

"Ready," she replied, holding her breath while he wiggled the big helmet over her head. He strapped the face guard in place, then stood back.

"You're a sight for sore eyes. What did you say your name was?"

"Lee. Lee . . . Brewer."

Mr. Brewer liked the idea of Molly using his name. She certainly couldn't use Maguire—the kids would put two and two together and come up with Molly, she knew. And Mr. Brewer was like a grandfather to her, so it felt natural to use his name.

She walked slowly along the sidewalk, careful not to step on any cracks. She didn't want to break her mother's back. After all, her mom was going to have a big enough shock when she found out Molly was playing football.

As she neared the park, she saw the boys doing wind sprints—running as fast as they could for a set distance. She was deliberately late. Mr. Brewer said that would be a good reason for arriving with her helmet on.

Molly took a deep breath and prayed, *Dear God, please don't let them find out it's me. And help me to run faster than anybody.* She ran out onto the grassy field and fell in with the team.

So far, so good. They had been running for fifteen minutes and she wasn't even winded, but some of the boys were huffing and puffing already. No one paid much attention to her. Some of the boys said "Hi" as they ran past, and she nodded in response.

Then the coach called out, "Over here, guys. Let's check your paperwork."

They lined up and Coach called their names. One by one, the boys handed in their registration forms.

"Brewer, Lee."

Molly gulped and went forward, holding out her papers.

Coach looked at her a minute, then said, "You looked fast out there. Keep it up."

Molly tried to melt into the group without calling attention to herself, but the coach's remark had made that difficult. Many of the boys looked openly curious.

"Where do you go to school? I haven't seen you around Lincoln Elementary," Bobby Stowe said.

Molly wanted to answer, *I sit one row over from you and you were my Kris Kringle last year*. Instead, she dropped her voice to a gravelly pitch and said, "I go to St. Raphael's. We don't have football, so I thought I'd try playing with the Parks and Recreation team."

"Is this your first year?" Ray Crowley asked. Ray had lived down the street from her all her life.

"Yeah," she said, looking at her sneaker. She had to remember to keep her voice low.

Ray's eyes followed hers. "Better get some cleats. Coach won't let you play in sneakers."

"Uh . . . Yeah." Molly hadn't thought about shoes. Would Jason recognize her blue tennies with her pinky toe poking out?

But Jason wasn't looking at her shoes. He was studying her face, or what he could see of it. She turned her head away from his stare.

"St. Rafael's?"

"Umhum. This is my fifth year."

"Kinda far from here, isn't it?"

"Not really. You get used to it." *Dear God, he's going to find out. Do something!*

"Hustle, hustle, hustle!" the coach was yelling, getting all the guys lined up for calisthenics.

"First, stretching exercises. Then, jumping jacks. Next, leg lifts. And before you go home today, you'll be pounding your bellies. Now hustle!"

Everyone was so intent on following Coach's orders, they forgot about Molly for the moment. She breathed more easily as she took her place and began the workout.

Half an hour later, Molly thought she would die of utter exhaustion. Her arms and legs were numb. She didn't think she could even stand up.

Then Coach said, "Pound your bellies, and I mean *pound!*"

Molly looked in disbelief as the boys pulled up their shirts and actually pounded themselves with their fists.

"You'll get used to it," Jason whispered.

Molly was not to be outdone. She pounded her

24

poor little tummy **real** hard until she didn't think it was possible to hurt anymore. Some of the boys didn't pull their shirts up, she noticed, so it didn't look too peculiar for her not to pull hers up, either.

"Good workout, guys. See you all tomorrow at four sharp," the coach said. "We'll be starting the meat grinder, so remember there's a reason for all this punishment. Eat plenty and get lots of sleep," he called over his shoulder as he walked to his car.

Molly sat in the cool grass, her arms wrapped around her knees. She couldn't move. The guys on the team slowly got their gear together and moved off in all directions, heading home.

Ray stopped in front of her. "Hey, Lee. Aren't you going home?"

"Yeah. I'm just catching my breath," she said in her gravel voice.

"See you tomorrow then," and Ray walked off swinging his helmet.

Soon the park was empty. Still Molly sat. It felt good just to sit. A fly buzzed around her head and she didn't even swat it. She heard birds chirping noisily, busily looking for their dinner. She heard car doors slam in the distance and children's voices welcoming their parents home from work.

Finally, Molly tried to unfold her tired, sore body. Was she crazy for trying to play football? Was it worth all this pain?

Chapter Five

Molly walked slowly into the house, unstrapping her helmet. Her mother turned from the stove, and her mouth fell open.

"What in the world . . . ? Molly, what are you doing dressed like that? And how did you get so dirty?"

Molly slumped into a chair.

"I'm playing football, Mom. That makes you dirty."

"Football? Since when do girls in Oak Glen play football?"

"Girls don't. I do. They don't know I'm a girl," Molly answered wearily.

"Who doesn't know you're a girl? Molly, what is this all about?"

"I wanted to play football, that's all. I wanted to show those dumb boys that girls are just as good, just as tough. Only . . ."

"Only what?"

"Only I'm not sure I'm as tough as I thought. I hurt all over."

Her mother looked at her closely, then shook her head.

"Get upstairs into a hot bath. We'll discuss this when your father gets home."

Oh oh. When Mom said "your father", it usually meant trouble.

Molly started up the stairs, taking them one at a time at a snail's pace.

She pulled off her uniform and filled the tub with hot water, then eased her aching body in. Her arms floated at the top of the water and her legs stretched out on the bottom. It felt so good just to lie there, eyes closed, and let the warm water work its miracle on her sore muscles. So peaceful . . .

"Molly, I'm going to kill you! Where are you, you little creep? After all I've done for you. Just wait until I get my hands on you, you, you *thief!* You *sneak!* You rotten little *toad!*"

Molly sat bolt upright in the tub, sloshing water over the edge and flooding the bathroom floor. Thank God she had locked the door.

"Are you in there?" Colleen screamed, beating on the door. "Answer me!"

"For Pete's sake, Col. What did I do?" Molly grabbed a towel and dried herself quickly. She pulled on her jeans and tee shirt and opened the door.

Colleen's usually creamy white skin was

27

blotched red with anger. Her eyes sparked furiously.

"Come with me," she said through gritted teeth.

Molly followed her into their shared bedroom, a knot forming in her stomach. She knew what the problem was, even before Colleen pointed at her dressing table.

The bottle of makeup base was tipped over, beige liquid oozing onto the table top. The blush brush was splayed open, bristles going every which way except flat. There was a gob of Vaseline smeared on the box of Kleenex and the mascara wand was out of its container, dried up and useless.

Colleen started to cry. "How could you do this to me? I tried so hard to help you out. Do you know how much all this stuff costs?"

"I'm really sorry, Colleen. Honest. I'll clean it all up, and you can have the five dollars Grandma sent me for my birthday to buy more stuff. Okay?"

Molly tried to wipe up the makeup base with some Kleenex and only succeeded in smearing it like finger paint all over the table.

"Honest. I'll clean it up," she said, hurrying to the bathroom for a wet washcloth.

Colleen sat quietly crying while Molly tried to undo the damage she had done early that morning. When she was finished, she sat next to Colleen on the bed.

"I really am sorry, Colleen. I didn't mean to make such a mess."

"Why were you using my makeup? Fifth graders don't use makeup."

"I know," Molly answered miserably. "I wanted to look pretty like you. That's all." Her voice was barely above a whisper.

Colleen didn't say anything at first. Then a tiny smile curved her lips. "Did you?" she asked. "Did you look pretty?"

Molly shook her head. "I thought I looked nice, but everyone laughed at me."

Colleen patted her on the knee. "Next time I'll help you. But don't you dare use my stuff without asking again."

"I won't. Promise. And don't tell Mom, okay?"

"All right."

"Are you still mad?"

"No. I really wasn't totally mad at you, anyway. I'm upset about something else, too."

"What?"

"It's high school stuff. You wouldn't understand."

"Try me."

Colleen studied her a minute, then said, "I like Mike Donovan and he took Melissa Patterson to Homecoming. I can't get it out of my mind. That's all I think about, and I just feel mad and like crying all the time."

Molly had never seen Colleen like this before. She was always so sure of herself. She always looked terrific. It seemed that everyone liked her. It was hard to believe she could get so upset just because some dumb boy took another girl to a dance.

"I don't know why you like him so much. He

must be blind or stupid or both to ask someone else when he could have taken you."

Colleen laughed. "Thanks," she said. "It's nice to have a loyal little sister."

"I mean it. Why do you like him so much if he's such a jerk?"

"He's not a jerk. He's cute. He has really beautiful green eyes with gold specks in them and . . ."

"That's his problem. He has specks in his eyes. No wonder he can't see you're prettier than Melissa Patterson."

"I wish. You should see Melissa Patterson. She's gorgeous."

"Okay. So he took Miss Gorgeous to the Homecoming dance. That was only one night. Maybe he'll ask you out another night."

"Maybe," Colleen said, but she didn't sound convinced.

Molly heard the front door slam and instantly felt her stomach drop to her toes. Dad was home!

She forgot Colleen's problem and began to think of ways to convince her parents she really should be allowed to play football, in spite of her aches and pains, in spite of her being a girl.

Chapter Six

Molly usually greeted her dad with a big hug when he came home from work, but tonight she was avoiding him. She stayed upstairs until her mother called her to set the table, but the moment came when she had to face him.

"Hi there, Pumpkin. Have a good day?" he asked, setting down his newspaper.

"It was okay."

"How did you do on your spelling test?"

"Only got two wrong."

"Which two?"

"Ceiling and believe."

"I before e . . ."

"Except after c. I know. I just forgot. I had a lot on my mind." As soon as the words were out of her mouth, Molly wanted to bite her tongue.

"Oh? Like what?"

"Nothing really. Mom's ready to dish up. I'd better go help."

"Colleen's helping. Sit down here and talk to me a minute."

Molly sat on the footstool by her father's chair. She studied the carpet with great interest.

"Molly," her dad said gently.

Slowly she looked up at him, at the warm smile and the twinkle in his eyes.

"Did Mom tell you?"

"Yes."

"Well? Am I grounded forever and ever?"

"I don't know. We haven't really discussed it yet. I'd like to hear all about it from the beginning. But first, let's eat."

Molly didn't think she'd be able to eat at all, but when a big plate of spaghetti was placed in front of her, she began to devour it.

"Mother, she's eating like a pig," Colleen complained.

Back to normal, thought Molly.

"Molly," her mother admonished. "Mind your manners."

"Football players have voracious appetites," Dad said, smiling.

"What's voracious?" Molly asked.

"It's one of the reasons you have a dictionary. Look it up," Dad answered.

Voracious. Voracious. I hope I can remember that until after dinner, thought Molly.

When the last plate was cleared away, her dad said, "Tell me about football, Molly. Is it fun?"

Molly had expected arguments, statements

questioning her sanity, static, but not that question. Fun? She thought a minute. "Not exactly. But it will be. As soon as I get used to it, I mean."

"Is it hard?"

"Yes. But not like school's hard. It's more like carrying-out-the-trash-cans hard. It's more like work."

"Do you have friends on the team?"

"I know most of the guys."

"That's not what I asked," her dad said gently. "Are any of them your friends?"

"Well," Molly stalled. How could she tell Dad about Jason and his dumb song, about the boys who laughed at her and Arabella and the other girls?

"Not really. At least," she added on a sudden inspiration, "not yet."

"Does that mean you want to be friends with these boys?"

"I guess. If they want to be friends with me."

"I see. What do they think about a girl playing football on their team?"

Molly hung her head. *Here it comes,* she thought. *Lecture number 213 on being honest at all costs.*

"They don't know."

Molly watched her fingers folding and unfolding a paper napkin. She was aware of the sounds of a neighbor cutting the grass and a dog barking. She was aware of her father's silence. Slowly, she looked up and her eyes locked with his.

"I never said I *wasn't* a girl. And I never said

33

I *was* a boy. Nobody asked," she added, defensively.

"I see."

"Daddy, please let me play. It means so much to me. And if it ever comes up about me being a girl, I won't lie. I promise."

"What if you get hurt? I know how rough boys can be. They'll mow right over you."

"With all those pads and turtles, I don't think I could ever get hurt. But I'll be real careful. Honest."

"Turtles? What in tarnation . . . ?"

"Part of my uniform. The part that goes on my shoulders. You know. Turtles."

"Yes. Of course. Turtles."

"And Dad, I need to get some cleats before practice tomorrow. Can you take me? I'm not allowed to wear sneakers."

Mr. Maguire sighed deeply, then smiled in resignation. "I'll see if Mom wants to go with us."

Yippee! I won! Molly thought, barely able to contain the happiness that threatened to spill from the inside out.

She still had laughter in her voice a moment later when the phone rang.

"Hello? Colleen . . . ? I think she's in the bathroom . . . she'll be a while. She always takes a long time. I think she's got a problem or something. No one else takes that long . . . Okay. Bye."

When she hung up the phone, Molly turned and saw Colleen standing in the doorway, her face white.

"Who was that?"

"I don't know. I forgot to ask. Just some boy."

"And you told him I was in the *bathroom?*"

"Yes. Weren't you?"

Colleen's face was turning red. *How does she do that,* Molly wondered.

"Don't ever tell anyone I'm in the bathroom. *Ever!* Understand?"

"Yeah, I guess. But won't people think you're a little weird if you never use the bathroom?"

"Get her out of here before I do something drastic!" Colleen hissed as their mother and father walked through the room to the front door.

"She should be an actress," Molly said, climbing into the back seat of the car. "She can change the color of her face real easy, and she sounds so good when she gets dramatic."

Her parents just looked at each other and shook their heads.

Molly wiggled happily into the corner of the seat. She had already forgotten Colleen's anger and was anticipating how wonderful her new cleats would look with her uniform.

Chapter Seven

September sun spilled through the window, flooding Molly's bed with light. Colleen was already in the shower, so Molly lay there a while longer, savoring the comfort of early morning. She looked at the sack on the floor by her closet. There they were, all ready for this afternoon. On impulse, Molly jumped out of bed and pulled a pair of socks on, then lifted the lid of the shoe box. Nestled toe to heel and wrapped in tissue paper were her brand new cleats.

She put them on, then walked slowly around the room. They really felt funny, like she was walking on ridges or something. They made her taller, too. She smiled in satisfaction.

"Good grief, you even *look* like a jock," Colleen said, walking into the room.

"Thanks," Molly said, smiling.

"I didn't mean it as a compliment."

"That's okay. I like being a jock."

"Weird," Colleen muttered, plugging in her curling iron.

At breakfast, Molly stirred milk and brown sugar into her oatmeal.

"How can you eat that junk?" Colleen asked, breaking a piece of dry toast into four neat squares.

"Me? How can you eat toast with no butter and jelly?"

"I'm on a diet."

"What for? You're already so skinny your bones stick out."

"Mother!"

"She's right, Colleen. You certainly don't need to be on a diet. And oatmeal is very nutritious."

"When *you're* not home, she pours syrup all over it. How nutritious is that?"

"Enough, girls. I don't like to start my day with squabbles, especially over oatmeal," their dad commented. "Colleen, you're beautiful just the way you are. You don't need to lose an ounce. And Molly, keep eating oatmeal. It's fuel for your body, and football players need lots of fuel."

He dropped a kiss on the top of Colleen's head and mussed Molly's hair playfully. "See you all tonight. If I can get home early, I'll stop by practice and watch you, Molly."

"Oh no! Please Dad, don't do that. You'd give me away."

"What if I came to watch Ray Crowley? You know, just casually dropped by?"

"I'd drop dead. Honest, Dad, I couldn't play if I knew you were there watching me. It would just be too suspicious."

"Okay, okay, I won't come. Not today, anyway. See you later."

"I don't believe it," Arabella said, shaking her head. "They didn't get mad and they bought you *cleats!* My folks would have hog-tied me to my bed for three months, but yours actually let you do it. Your mom and dad are terrific."

"Yeah, I know," Molly agreed. They had almost reached school when Jason came up behind them on his bike. He screeched on his brakes and skidded, his front wheel hitting the back of Molly's leg.

"Ow! Watch where you're going, you creep!"

"I'm watching. Too bad you're just a sissy girl. A football player wouldn't have even felt that little tap."

"Oh yeah?"

"Yeah!"

Molly's blood was boiling, but she didn't dare say another word.

Arabella looked at her anxiously. She knew Molly had a hard time keeping her mouth shut.

Arabella was right.

"What do *you* know about football players, Jason?"

"I'm on the team, so there."

38

"Which team is that? The International Team of Klutzes and Dweebs?"

By this time they were at school and the first bell had rung. Molly and Arabella ran up the steps while Jason pushed his bike into the bike rack. Molly knew Jason was fuming, but she didn't care. She had gotten the last word in this time.

All during math, penmanship, and spelling Molly felt smug. She smiled secretly to herself. It was wonderful to get the best of Jason.

Arabella passed her a note. "Let's make warts!"

Molly nodded then reached under her desk for her lunch bag. She quietly tore a small corner off the brown bag and put it in her lap. Watching Miss Bloom, she tore the paper into tiny bits, putting each bit into her mouth and wetting it with spit. Then she rolled the tiny brown wad between her fingers and stuck the "wart" on her arm. She had eight warts on her arms and the last one she stuck on the tip of her nose. Miss Bloom hadn't noticed any of this, but Arabella did all she could to keep from laughing out loud when Molly crossed her eyes. Luckily, the recess bell rang before Arabella split herself in two from trying to hold in her laughter.

Molly heard Jason, who had been especially quiet all morning, begin to laugh, too. Softly at first, then louder as his buddies got next to him in line. Arabella fell in next to Molly, and her smiling face suddenly became horrified.

"What's wrong?" asked Molly.

"Your hair," Arabella whispered. "It's been tied into a thousand knots!"

By this time they were outside and Jason and his friends were howling.

Molly put her hand to her head. Her hair had been twisted and thin strands were tied into real knots all over the back of her head. It was horrible!

"He must have spent the whole morning doing that," Arabella said in dismay. She looked at Molly critically, head tipped to one side. "At least he left the front and sides alone. If the other girls will help, we can undo it before recess is over."

Arabella recruited Jennifer, Sara, and Lisa. Molly sat still while they tugged and untwisted, but the job still wasn't finished when the bell rang. And the hair on the back of Molly's head stuck out like a porcupine's quills.

She had spent the whole recess trying to think of a way to rid the world of Jason Jenson once and for all, but nothing came to her short of murder.

By lunch time, Molly had a gargantuan headache. Even her PB and J didn't help.

Miss Bloom took her to the office and Old Beetlenose, the secretary, gave her a Tylenol.

"If your head still hurts in half an hour, I'll call your mother. You may as well be home in your bed as suffering through the rest of the day here," Beetlenose said. In spite of her lumpy nose and unattractive face, Beetlenose was really nice.

"I'm sure I'll feel better," Molly said, knowing

full well she wouldn't be allowed to play football after school if she was sent home sick.

In ten minutes she asked to go back to class.

"Hey, Red, where do you get your hair done? The Electric Company?" Jason whispered when she sat down. "It looks like you put your finger in a socket."

By this time Molly's head hurt so badly she didn't care what Jason said, so she just ignored him.

"What's the matter, Carrot Top? Cat got your tongue?"

She didn't reply.

> *"Freckle face, freckle face,*
> *Brown muddy spots.*
> *Freckle face, freckle face,*
> *Molly grows her hair in pots."*

"Jason, will you please pay attention? I asked you to name the capital of Uruguay."

"Uh, Uh, Paraguay?"

"No. Uruguay."

"Uh, I'm not sure."

"Then take a guess." Miss Bloom looked mad.

"Lima?"

"Good grief, Jason!" Miss Bloom *was* mad. "Haven't you been listening to any of our social studies class? Tonight I want you to write me a full page report on Uruguay. And include the capital."

The sound of muffled laughter erupted as the girls showed their approval of Jason's punishment.

Molly grinned. For some reason, her head felt a little better now. She could even look forward to football practice after school.

Chapter Eight

After school, Molly got her gear and went over to Mr. Brewer's house. She noticed for the hundredth time how nice his house smelled. Colleen always complained that Mr. Brewer's house smelled musty and like an old man, but Molly liked the smell. Sort of pipe tobacco-y mixed with coffee and onions. Her own house smelled like furniture polish and soap because her mother was always cleaning. Frankly, Molly couldn't see anything wrong with a little dirt and grime—it showed someone was having fun. But her mom liked everything shiny clean, so dust balls and dirt didn't have much chance to move in and make themselves at home. Mr. Brewer's house was a pleasant change.

"Hurry up, Girl. Got to get you ready for football practice. Did you get your cleats?"

"Last night. They're really neat," she said, proudly showing him.

He helped her as he had before, but she was getting used to her uniform and how to get into it. Besides, Mr. Brewer seemed to tire easily and had to sit down.

"Must be getting old," he mumbled.

"That's okay. I can do it. Besides, I have to learn sometime," Molly said cheerfully, tucking her hair into the white cotton cap.

"Guess so," Mr. Brewer said, rubbing his arm.

"Gotta go now. See you later."

"Better make it tomorrow. I'm going to bed early tonight."

"Right. See you."

"Come on, Lee. You're late," Coach called from the practice area. Molly ran her fingers under her helmet to make sure her hair was tucked in securely, adjusted her goggles, then ran out with the team. They were doing wind sprints and she fell in with ease. Practice followed the same course it had the previous day. Leg lifts, jumping jacks, and stretching exercises.

Molly was sore, but not as bad as before. She got into the calisthenics with all her energy and felt really good doing them.

Then Coach handed out the play book. He explained the different plays, using diagrams. He talked about a new practice drill, one they hadn't done yet. The meat grinder. Molly felt her face blanch as Coach described it.

"We'll use two blocking dummies with a man

holding each one. You'll run the ball between the dummies and try not to get creamed. Of course, the purpose of the guys holding the dummies is to cream you and this will prepare you for taking a hit during a game."

Oh boy, oh boy, she thought. *I may just get killed.*

"We'll use dummies for blocking and tackling until you learn the techniques," Coach was saying. "And I don't want any full contact until next week. By the way, it goes without saying, I won't tolerate any fighting. This is football, not boxing. I don't want to hear you tell me you punched out a kid from another team because he punched you first. It's against the rules for ANY reason. AND, don't grab anyone's facemask. Got it?"

"We hear you," Ray Crowley said.

"I wish Dozer could hear him," whispered Bobby Stowe.

"Who's Dozer?" Molly asked.

"A guy on the Lancers. He's the dirtiest player I've ever seen. He's a big bully. Dozer is short for bulldozer."

Molly gulped. "Will we be playing the Lancers?"

"First game is in two weeks. Against the Lancers."

Molly shivered. "We'd better practice hard so we can beat them."

"You're not kidding." Bobby was just as scared as she was.

Half an hour later, Molly was facing her first meat grinder. She supposed it was fitting that

45

the first grinder she'd face was with Jason. She had to remember to keep her head low so he wouldn't have a chance to recognize her in such close contact. She gripped the ball tightly against her side, dug her cleats into the spongy grass, and started running with all her might.

"Both hands, Lee! Carry with both hands!" Coach yelled.

Molly pulled her left arm across her right, hugging the football, and plowed ahead. Jason was braced and ready to knock her for a loop, as was Ray, holding the dummy right next to him. She kept going, knowing she was in for it but still surprised when they hit. The crash of two big dummies knocked the wind out of her and sent her flying across the turf. She was dazed for a minute, tasting the grit of dirt and grass and feeling numb. The numbness was temporary. Very temporary. It was replaced by a severe aching in her chest, stomach, arms and legs.

"You okay, Lee?"

Coach was standing over her, stretching out a hand to help her up.

"I'm fine. Just winded." *Darn,* she thought. *I forgot to drop my voice. Wonder if he noticed?*

Coach turned to tell the next boy how he should run the grinder, so Molly decided she was safe for now. She kept her head lowered and stood on the sidelines watching the other kids take their turns. Football was not an easy sport. She was beginning to have a grudging respect for these boys who worked so hard to be good at it.

When practice was over, Molly sat down on the

grass to catch her breath. It had been hard on her, but she had hung in there and managed to keep up. One thing she knew for sure—she was the fastest runner on the team. And that felt good.

Surprisingly, Jason came and sat next to her.

"Where do you live?" he asked.

"Not far," she answered vaguely, this time remembering to lower her voice. "I'm going to my grandad's."

"Oh. Hey, can I ask you something?"

Molly's throat tightened. "Sure," she said.

"How come you never take your helmet off?"

Oh Lord, help me think.

"You're not going to believe this," she began. "My sister dyed my hair purple and I had to shave it off."

Jason laughed. "I'd kill her," he said.

"I did," Molly answered.

Then Jason's forehead wrinkled and a small river of sweat ran down the side of his face. He didn't look happy.

"What's the matter?" Molly asked.

"I've got a dumb social studies paper to do tonight. All on account of a dumb girl."

What! It wasn't *her* fault he kept needling her and got in trouble! The jerk.

"What happened?" she asked casually, turning her head away from him.

"This Molly who sits in front of me at school. She's always getting me in trouble. She's got red hair and you know what *that* means."

"No, I don't. What does it mean?" Molly couldn't

47

believe it was her gravelly voice that sounded so unconcerned. She wanted to clobber Jason!

"They're always so hyper. You know. She's always doing stuff and then I get blamed. She's smart, too. Thinks she knows it all."

"No kidding." *What a turkey!*

"Yeah. But I got her last week. I stole her homework," Jason said, laughing wickedly.

Molly was bristling. Her goggles felt tight against her face and her helmet was heavy. She'd give anything to be able to take them off. And her neck was getting stiff from trying to keep her head turned halfway sideways so Jason couldn't look right at her face. But she almost forgot her discomfort when he admitted he took her homework. He was really pushing it.

"Did she get in trouble?"

"Yeah. Had to do it over at lunch time. But just wait until next week," he said, eyes gleaming.

"Why?"

"Our class is going on a skating party at Skate City. And boy, is she going to get it."

"What are you going to do?" Molly kept her voice low, but her curiosity almost caused her to look Jason square in the eye. She recovered in an instant and turned her head.

Jason didn't seem to notice.

"My dad has some kind of special Super Glue. I'm going to glue her skate wheels together," he said grinning. "Then watch her splat!"

"Just because she's smart?"

"Aw, she's always doing stuff. Thinks she's as tough as a boy. My dad says girls like that should

48

be put in their place. She's the kind of girl who thinks she should be able to drive a truck or be an astronaut. You know."

"Yeah," Molly said, almost choking on the word. The *nerve* of that creep!

"My dad says girls should stay home and learn to cook. That's their place."

Molly was steaming. She felt her fists clench and her face get hot. She almost bit off the words that tumbled from her lips. "What does your dad think of girls who play football?"

Jason hooted. "You're kidding," he said. "Heck, everybody knows girls can't play football. Can you imagine some dumb girl going through the meat grinder? She'd get creamed in a second."

Molly's chin shot out. "I heard of a girl who plays on a high school team in Detroit."

"Sure. My dad says her folks *paid* the coach to let her play."

Molly stood up. She had had enough. There was no way she could continue being civil to this jerk.

"Gotta go," she mumbled through white lips.

"Hey, wait a sec," Jason called after her. "Do you happen to know the capital of Uruguay?"

Molly turned slightly and muttered, "I think it's Lima," then continued walking. *Let the creep find out it's Montevideo on his own. I hope he never finds it!*

Chapter Nine

Molly walked aimlessly. She didn't want to go home just yet and she felt like talking. Finally, she decided to go to Arabella's house. Sometimes she could talk to Arabella and find answers to her problems, even if Arabella didn't say a word.

"I wondered if you were ever going to stop by and show me your uniform," Arabella said when she opened the door. "It looks great!" Her eyes sparkled mischievously. "Has anyone guessed yet?"

"No. So far so good."

"That's funny. I can tell it's you. I wonder why the boys can't?"

"Because I'm the last person they would expect to see out there, for one thing. You *know* it's me, but they think I'm just a guy from another school. And," Molly added, dropping her voice, "I talk like this when I'm with them."

Arabella howled. "That's perfect! You're too much, Molly. Come on up to my room. I don't want Mom to see you and have a stroke. She doesn't know yet."

Arabella's room was pretty and pink and frilly. Molly felt self-conscious sitting on the eyelet bedspread in her grungy uniform. She squirmed and tried to have just the smallest part of her bottom on the bed, letting her arms and legs dangle over the side, not touching anything.

"For Pete's sake, Molly. Do you think my bed has cooties or something?"

"It's me. I'm all dirty."

"So what? That spread will wash. Here," she added, bending deep into her closet and retrieving a small tin cookie can. "Have a brownie."

"I *love* brownies. Especially with lots of frosting. Why are they in your closet?"

"Because the Nerd eats the whole pan every time Mom makes them. I have to get my own supply and hide them."

The Nerd was Arabella's eight-year-old brother, Harry. He was a real pest.

Molly forgot about her dirty pants and got comfortable sitting crosslegged on Arabella's bed.

"Can you help me with my math?" Arabella asked. "I just get lost subtracting thousands. All those zeros make me think of ants on spilled jelly—they just go on and on."

"Sure. I love math. Isn't it funny how I love math and you love English? It's a good thing, too.

51

If we both loved the same subject we couldn't help each other with the one we weren't good at, and we'd both probably flunk."

"I guess," Arabella said, looking like she didn't really understand at all. "Before we haul out the books, though, tell me about football."

"I *love* football! I . . ."

"You love everything," Arabella interrupted.

"No, I don't. I don't love English and I don't love Jason. Honestly, he's such a jerk."

"What did he do now?"

Molly told Arabella all about her conversation with Jason after football practice. "Can you believe that? It's all *my* fault he has to write about Uruguay."

"What do you expect from such a dweeb? I'll bet he stinks at football, too," Arabella said, nodding her head expectantly.

Molly was thoughtful, then said, "He's good at football. And he's very nice to me. I mean me as Lee, not me as Molly. But he has such old-fashioned ideas of what girls should and shouldn't do. It's so unbelievable it's almost a joke.".

"Maybe he doesn't know better," Arabella said, stuffing another brownie in her mouth.

"He *must* know better. Anyone with any brains at all would know better."

Molly and Arabella looked at each other, then they both burst out laughing.

"There's your answer," Arabella said. "He has no brains!"

* * *

When Molly got home she expected to see Colleen primping in front of the mirror, but she wasn't home yet so Molly stripped off her football gear and soaked in a hot tub. She'd have to talk to Colleen about Jason later.

It was almost dinnertime when she went downstairs clean and hungry.

Colleen floated through the door ten minutes later. Her face was wreathed in smiles and she looked so dreamy Molly thought she was going to throw up.

"What happened to you? Did you meet Tom Cruise or something?"

Colleen continued to smile. She didn't even say anything nasty to Molly.

"Mike Donovan walked me home. And you were right, Molly. He asked me out."

"No kidding. He finally got his eyes fixed, huh?"

"He said he's been noticing me for a long time. He said he used to sit in the cafeteria and watch me eat my lunch. He's so romantic."

"Yeah, there's nothing like a bologna sandwich to bring out the romance in someone. Did he tell you about how he watched Melissa Patterson, too? Did he tell you why he didn't ask you to Homecoming?"

"Molly Maguire, that's enough!" her mother exploded. "How can you be so unkind to your sister? Go on, dear," she said to Colleen.

"There's not much else. We're going to a movie tomorrow night, that's all." Then Colleen turned the full radiance of her smile on Molly.

"He wants to meet you, Molly. He says any girl who plays football has to be extraordinary. That's the word he used. Extraordinary. So be cool tomorrow night when he comes over, will you? It means so much to me."

Molly's mouth was hanging open. "You *told* him? You actually *told* him?"

Colleen's smile was warm and sweet. "Why not? I'm proud of you, you know."

"You *creep!*" Molly screamed and ran up the stairs in tears.

Chapter Ten

Traitor. That's what she was. A traitor. She *knew* it was supposed to be a secret. Colleen *knew* she wasn't supposed to tell anyone. How could she do it? How could she tell Mike Donovan that Molly was playing football on the boy's team?

Molly punched her pillow savagely. It was bad enough having Jason for an enemy. Now she had Colleen, too.

She rolled over on top of her bed, wiping at tears that refused to stay in her eyes. *Doggone it!*

Finally, she sat up and blew her nose. She wrapped her arms around her knees and held her breath, trying to stop crying. It didn't work. The tears kept coming.

Molly sniffled and looked out the bedroom window, watching the moon chase the shadows in the old maple tree.

She looked down into Mr. Brewer's lighted kitchen and watched him shuffle from the table over to the counter.

As she watched, the tears on her cheeks dried. It suddenly dawned on Molly that something was wrong. Mr. Brewer was hanging on to the counter, his head bent. He didn't move.

She was off her bed and down the stairs like a shot. She didn't stop to tell her parents where she was going, but raced through the hedge and up Mr. Brewer's porch.

"Mr. Brewer," she gasped, running through the door without knocking. "Mr. Brewer, what's wrong?"

Molly's breath came in ragged spurts as she stood in the middle of the kitchen, unsure what to do next.

Mr. Brewer had slumped to the floor. His eyes were closed, and it looked as if he was having a hard time breathing.

Finally, his eyelids fluttered open and he recognized Molly.

"Doctor," he whispered with great effort. "Get doctor."

Molly stood staring for a long moment. Her heart was pounding like a jackhammer and she felt like her feet were stuck in cement.

Then she realized Mr. Brewer needed a doctor more than anything else in the world. Her fingers trembled as she dialed the number posted by the phone and her heart turned over when she heard the busy signal.

She dashed down the steps and the wind pulled

at her hair as she raced along the sidewalk, skipping over curbs and crossing streets with abandon for three blocks until she reached Dr. Wilson's house. She made it in record time, knowing full well her legs would carry her more swiftly than it would have taken to get her dad and the car.

"Dr. Wilson," she yelled, banging on the door with one hand and ringing the bell with the other.

The porch light was turned on somewhere inside the house and the door opened.

"Who's there?"

"It's me, Molly Maguire. Come quick. Mr. Brewer's all blue and very sick. Please, please hurry. I'm afraid he's going to die."

The fear that had clutched her heart ever since she saw Mr. Brewer hanging onto the counter from her bedroom window was finally put into words.

"I'm afraid he's going to die," she said again, slowly, quietly, listening to herself say the strange words.

"I'll get my bag," the doctor said, disappearing into the house. He was back in a second. "Well, come on," he said, shaking Molly.

She got into the car next to Dr. Wilson, noticing how cold the seat felt and how the smell of pipe tobacco clung to his clothes. Just like Mr. Brewer's.

"He won't die, will he?" she asked in a small voice.

"Not if I can help it." Dr. Wilson drove fast, his big hands expertly guiding the car.

In moments they were in Mr. Brewer's kitchen. Dr. Wilson bent over him, giving him oxygen to breathe from a green tank with a plastic tube that went around his neck and into his nose. Molly watched fearfully.

Then she felt her dad's warm hand on her shoulder and looked around to see her mom and Colleen standing behind her.

"What happened?" Colleen asked. "We heard tires screeching, and when we looked outside you and Dr. Wilson were running up the steps."

Tires screeching? Molly hadn't even noticed that.

"What happened?" Colleen asked again.

"He's real sick," Molly said.

Dr. Wilson rocked back on his heels to a sitting position and pulled the stethoscope out of his ears.

"Looks like Mr. Brewer's had a heart attack. We'll need to get him to the hospital," he said, going to the phone to call the ambulance.

Molly kept looking at Mr. Brewer lying on the floor with that plastic tube in his nose. He wasn't breathing so hard now and he wasn't blue anymore, but he still looked terrible. Molly had never seen him lying down with his eyes closed before. *Maybe that's why he looks so awful,* she thought. But she had seen her dad lying down with his eyes closed and he still looked normal. Mr. Brewer didn't look normal.

Dear God, please don't let him die.

Molly thought she had cried out all her tears earlier, but there was still one stubborn tear that refused to stay where it belonged and slid right out of her eye and down her cheek. Then another followed, and another. Soon her whole body was shaking and she was crying like a baby.

Her dad's strong arms gathered her close to him, warm and protected.

"It's okay, Pumpkin. Go ahead and cry."

Molly felt like a two-year-old bawling her head off, but it sure felt good and safe to have her dad's arms around her. By the time the ambulance came, she had blown her nose for the hundredth time and her eyes had dried up.

The ambulance men wheeled a narrow bed into the kitchen and lifted Mr. Brewer onto it. They tucked a blanket around him and started for the door.

Molly watched everything they did. She practically held her breath so she wouldn't miss anything.

When they wheeled Mr. Brewer past her, Molly was surprised to see his hand come out from under the blanket and reach for hers.

The ambulance men stopped and Molly held Mr. Brewer's hand tightly, trying to let him know through her touch how special he was to her.

"Hang in there, Girl. I'll be there for your first game, so practice hard." Then he winked and the ambulance men took him away.

Chapter Eleven

Molly's heart lifted and, for the first time in the last hour, she felt hope. Real hope. Mr. Brewer might not look normal, but he sure sounded normal. If he said he'd be there for her first game, he'd be there.

She went back home with her family and sat at the table for a cup of hot chocolate. The excitement and sadness she had experienced this evening were enough to last her a lifetime.

"How're you doing, Pumpkin? Feel washed out?" her dad asked.

"I guess so. I just feel numb right now. He's going to be all right, isn't he? He said he'd come to my game."

"I hope so. But we can't be sure, Molly. We'll just have to wait and see." Her dad stirred the melted marshmallow into his hot chocolate until it disappeared entirely. "Mom and I will go to the hospital first thing in the morning. We'll try to find out all we can."

"Tomorrow? What about work? Aren't you going to work?"

"Tomorrow's Saturday, Pumpkin," her dad said gently.

"Oh yeah. I forgot." Molly's head was spinning. All she could think about was Mr. Brewer lying helpless on the kitchen floor.

"Did you tell her what Dr. Wilson said?" her mother asked.

Molly's head came up. She hoped it wasn't something horrible about Mr. Brewer.

"Don't look so scared," her dad said, taking her hand in his. "Dr. Wilson told your mom and me that you probably saved Mr. Brewer's life."

Saved his life? "How?" Nothing was making sense to Molly.

"You got Dr. Wilson there so fast," Colleen answered. "If you hadn't found Mr. Brewer when you did and run as fast as you ran, he might not have made it."

"That's right," her dad agreed. "Your fast legs probably saved his life."

Molly looked around the table at her family. Her mother was smiling, her dad nodded his head. Colleen looked the way she always did when they weren't fighting, like she was Molly's best friend in the whole world.

"Really?"

"Yes, really."

"Of course."

They all spoke at once and Molly finally understood. Her action got the doctor to Mr. Brewer when there were only minutes to spare. A slow smile spread over her face.

"No kidding." She thought about all the wind sprints she had been doing at football practice, all the hard exercises. They had paid off. Even if she never made a touchdown, all the grueling practice had paid off. It got her in shape to help Mr. Brewer when he needed it the most. And that was worth everything.

The next morning her parents kept their word and went to the hospital right after breakfast. Colleen seemed anxious to get her weekly jobs done and had the dust rag and vacuum cleaner going at full speed.

Molly wandered from room to room, knowing she had to clean the bathroom but putting it off. She didn't feel like doing anything. She just wanted her parents to come home and say Mr. Brewer was fine and she could go see him.

The phone rang.

Molly's heart dropped to her toes. Maybe Mr. Brewer wasn't doing well. Maybe . . . she stifled the thought.

"Hello?" Her voice sounded shaky.

"Hi. Done with your job yet?"

"Huh?"

"Are you finished with your Saturday job yet?"

Arabella spoke slowly and deliberately. "What's the matter with you, Molly? Are you sick?"

"No, but Mr. Brewer is," she answered and told Arabella what had happened last night.

"Why don't you come over to my house? The Nerd is going out to Taylor's Woods with the Cub Scouts. We'll have the place to ourselves. Maybe we could bake something."

That did sound better to Molly than moping around her house. "I'll do the bathroom, then I'll be over. See 'ya."

Molly scoured and scrubbed and polished. The bathroom was clean in five minutes. Colleen came in as she was collecting the dirty towels and washcloths to take downstairs to the utility room.

"On no, you don't," she said, sounding a lot like their mother. "You didn't clean the toilet. I can tell. Get busy."

"What's wrong with it?" Even Molly could see the water line in the bowl, but she played innocent.

"Come on, Molly, don't give me that. Do it. And please do a good job. Mike's coming tonight to pick me up, remember? You never know. He may just need to use the bathroom."

Mike! Molly had forgotten all about her fight with Colleen over Colleen telling Mike she played football. That seemed so long ago.

"Well, I'll be sure to put a spit shine on the toilet," Molly said, "just in case Mr. Wonderful has to pee!"

*   *   *

Molly was heading down the driveway on her bike when her parents pulled up in the car. She dropped her bike. "Well? How is he? Can I go see him?"

"He's doing very well, Pumpkin. Dr. Wilson says he'll be able to come home next week, probably. But he needs lots of rest now. And no visitors. I'm sorry," her dad said, giving her a hug. "I know how badly you want to go see him, but they don't let anyone in the hospital under twelve to visit, even if he could have company. You'll have to think of something nice to do for him from home."

"What about you and Mom? Can you go see him?"

"Tomorrow, the doctor said. We'll go after church."

"Good. I'll have something for you to take by then."

Molly and Arabella surveyed the kitchen. There were white clouds of flour covering every surface. The countertops were scratchy with wet, spilled sugar. Melted butter had boiled over in the little pan, leaving a runny brown river under the burners on the stove. There were light brown clumps of cookie dough sticking to the walls and cupboards from when Arabella had lifted the mixer out of the bowl at full speed.

"Almost done," Molly said, licking a spoon. "All we have to do is stick the chocolate chips in the cookies."

"Get ready with the chips. Here they come,"

Arabella said, opening the oven door with a pot holder. The girls studied the cookies—some small and dark, others fat and light, all with rather black bottoms.

"They don't look like my mother's," Molly groaned.

"They'll look better when we get the chocolate chips in," Arabella replied.

The girls were busy pressing chocolate chips into the baked cookies when Arabella's mother walked in. She didn't say a word, just looked at the mess. Her face got as white as the spilled flour and she clamped her mouth shut tight, then turned and walked out.

"I think we have to clean up," Arabella said.

"I think you're right," Molly answered. "It sure was nice of your mom to let us bake cookies for Mr. Brewer. I know he'll love these," she added with satisfaction, looking at the plate of lumpy, pitted cookies, mostly broken, mostly burnt.

"Yeah. Only next time, let's remember to put the chips in *before* we bake them."

They both giggled.

Molly heard the doorbell ring and realized too late who it was. *Mike.*

Colleen, of course, was in the bathroom, and her mom and dad were out back talking to a neighbor about Mr. Brewer.

She'd have to answer the door, even though she wanted to avoid Mike. It would be just her luck that he'd blab to the whole world about her playing football.

She opened the door.

"Come in, Mike. You *are* Mike, aren't you?"

"Yes, and you're Molly. I'm happy to meet you," he said, putting out his hand.

No one ever shook Molly's hand before. She felt a little taller and a little more grown up.

"Colleen will be right down. She's in the . . ." *Oh oh, don't say the B word,* she told herself. " . . . the upstairs room where you brush your teeth and stuff."

Mike grinned.

"So," he said. "Are you really playing football?"

"Yes, but you have to promise on your grandmother's grave you won't tell a soul," Molly said.

"I promise, though my grandmother will be surprised to hear she's dead. Why the big secret?" He was smiling a very warm smile.

"The boys don't know I'm a girl. And if they find out, well, I'll never be able to prove to them that I'm just as good and just as tough as they are. Especially *one* boy."

"I see," Mike said solemnly. "Your secret is safe with me."

He didn't laugh or make fun of her. Molly found herself liking this boy who'd broken Colleen's heart then mended it.

She stood toe to toe with him, then put her hands on his shoulders and got up on her tip toes so she could look into his eyes.

"Molly Maguire, what are you doing?" Colleen's horrified voice came from the doorway.

"Looking for the gold specks. I don't see any,"

she added, getting down and heading for the kitchen. She turned to tell them to have fun, but kept her mouth shut when she saw the look on Colleen's face.

Mike was shaking with laughter.

Chapter Twelve

Dear Molly,

I just finished four of the best cookies I've ever eaten in my life. I would have polished off all of them, but the nurse took them away until later. She said they weren't good for me right now. She doesn't know that the cookies you baked with your own two hands are the best medicine in the world for me. Besides being stuffed with chocolate chips, I know they're stuffed with love.

Being in the hospital is no darn fun at all. There's a crabby old man next to me who snores all the time, and the head nurse is about as attractive as a bucket of lard. There is a nice student nurse, though. She reminds me of you—sort of freckled and sweet as a speckled puppy in the springtime. I call her "Girl" and she laughs. She doesn't know that's the nicest thing I could possibly call her 'cause it's what I call you, and I hold you in more esteem than anyone else in the whole world.

I wonder if you know the old Indian saying that when you save a person's life, that person now belongs to you. Think about it, Girl. I'm all yours! Now whatever are you going to do with me?!

The doctor says I can move out of Intensive Care and into a regular room with a phone on Tuesday. Then I can call you and we can have us a nice long talk.

Until then, old Lard Bucket is making me take a nap—you'd think I was three years old!

Thanks for being there, Girl.

Mr. B.

Molly folded the letter for the twentieth time and slipped it under her pillow. When her folks came home from the hospital with it, she was overjoyed. Mr. Brewer's letter sounded just like Mr. Brewer. Not scary at all. She had been so afraid that the heart attack would have made him different somehow, but he didn't sound different. Her mom said he was still pale and a little peaked looking, but much better. And in two days she could talk to him.

Molly stretched under the covers, waiting for Colleen to turn the light off. She was still sitting in front of the mirror brushing her hair, looking sort of dreamy eyed at herself.

"Did you have fun on your date with Mike last night?" Molly asked, knowing the answer by looking at Colleen's face, but feeling she should ask anyway.

"Oh yes. Wonderful."

"Did he kiss you goodnight?"

"Yes. That was *really* wonderful."

"Yuk! How could kissing a boy be wonderful?"

Colleen turned around facing Molly. "It really is, Molly. It's hard to explain. But when you like someone a lot you just feel like you want to kiss him."

"I like Mr. Brewer a lot but I don't want to kiss him. I like Arabella's dog a lot, but I don't want to kiss him, either."

"That's different. When you like a boy in a *special* way—well, that's what I'm talking about. Look, well—don't you like Jason a little?"

"*Jason!*" Molly exploded. "Heck no! He's the biggest jerk. I'd *never* like him. In fact, I can't stand him. If I had to kiss him I'd throw up."

Colleen smiled. "Forget I said anything, okay? We'll talk about this some more in a couple of years. Good night," she said, turning off the light.

Molly tossed and turned for a half hour. *Kiss Jason! Oh Yuk! Just thinking about it makes*

me want to puke. How disgusting. Yuk! Yuk!
She finally fell into a fitful sleep.

The next morning during math Molly was multiplying 365×79 when she remembered her talk with Colleen the night before. She squirmed in her seat knowing Jason was sitting right behind her, and she felt the hot blush creep up her neck and stain her ears all red. *Wouldn't it be awful if he could read my mind?* she thought. The blush deepened. She couldn't concentrate on math. She couldn't even think clearly.

"Molly, will you please work the problem on the board for us? I see some people having trouble," Miss Bloom said.

What an awful time to get called on! Molly walked slowly to the board, trying desperately to put Jason out of her mind. She wrote the numbers with a new stick of chalk and, almost without thinking, she worked the problem. It had become automatic. Her fingers formed the numbers and part of her brain just took over. The answer, 28,835, appeared almost magically.

She turned from the board and started back to her seat, looking squarely at Jason.

Jason was looking at the board with a frown on his face, studying the problem. He didn't get it. Molly noticed his hair was dirty and uncombed. His papers were all messy on his desk. There was black grime under his fingernails.

Slowly, she smiled to herself. *There is no way in the world I'd ever want to kiss that boy, so I guess I don't have to be embarrassed. Colleen is really nuts.*

When she got back to her seat she reached under her desk and pulled out the little bottle of perfume Miss Bloom had given her. She held it tightly so no one else could see it. Just the feel of it gave her a sense of power. Something special no one else had. Something all her own. Something grown up. And right now, this very minute, she felt grown up. She unscrewed the lid and tipped the bottle so the perfume poured out on her finger. Just a little, Miss Bloom had said. Her finger slipped and suddenly perfume was pouring down her arm!

"Ugh! What's that horrible smell?" Jason sputtered.

All the kids whose desks were around Molly turned to stare at her. Jason was gagging and choking behind her. Even Arabella looked at her with a deep frown. Miss Bloom's eyebrows were practically in her hair, but she didn't say anything.

Molly's fingers felt like clubs trying to screw the lid back on the little bottle of perfume. She didn't feel very grown up anymore. Her ears were burning again and she knew her face was beet red.

"What are you trying to do? Kill us all with germ warfare?" Jason hissed.

"Not everybody. Just you!" she snapped over

her shoulder, wishing she could crawl under a board someplace. One thing was for sure. She'd never be like her beautiful grown-up sister, Colleen.

Chapter Thirteen

At recess Molly had gone into the bathroom and scrubbed her hands and arms. When she got home from school, she scrubbed again. But the stubborn odor of perfume clung to her. Just when she thought it was gone, Molly turned her head and got another whiff.

Darn! I can't go to practice like this, she thought.

She sat at the little table in the kitchen, her chin in her hand, trying to decide what to do. She couldn't think of a thing.

She looked around the room. Stove, refrigerator, sink, cupboards, pantry, countertops . . . vegetables. There on the counter was a pile of fresh vegetables all ready to be chopped and added to the stew simmering on the stove. Carrots, celery, rutabagas, potatoes, tomatoes, onions . . . *onions!*

They always smell so strong, she thought, jumping up and getting out a sharp knife and cutting board. She peeled and halved two large yellow onions, then began rubbing the cut sides on her arms, hands, neck, and face. Her eyes were streaming with onion tears, but Molly was smiling. She had finally gotten rid of the perfume smell!

"Move it!" Coach yelled, and the team fell into position.

"Yuk! What's that smell?" Bobby Stowe asked, his face all scrunched up.

"Phew. I can't stand it," Ray Crowley agreed.

"What stinks?" echoed Jason.

"Me," Molly replied in her gravelly voice.

"Why don't you take a bath then?" Bobby asked.

"It's not that. It's onions," Molly answered.

"Onions? What the heck for?" Jason asked.

"Virility. Haven't you ever heard onions are good for virility?"

"Vir . . . What's that?" asked Ray.

"Virility. You know, *macho.* Don't you want to be macho?"

"Sure I do. But I don't want to smell as bad as you do," Ray answered.

"You only smell this way the first day. After that, the odor goes inside you and makes you really strong. *Macho,*" Molly lied.

"No kidding? You mean if we eat an onion, we'll smell bad one day, then after that we'll be stronger?" Jason asked.

"Yep." Then Molly added, "Most people just rub it on their skin, but you get the *best* results from eating them. They'll make you strong. Sometimes it only takes a little while, not a whole day."

"Hmmmm. Maybe I'll try it," Ray said.

"Let me know how it works," Bobby said.

Jason started laughing. "I can just see Miss Bloom's face if you come in smelling like Lee does now. As if Molly's perfume today wasn't bad enough! Miss Bloom will think the whole fifth grade is trying to stink her out of the school!"

"Get moving, you guys. We have a game a week from Saturday and you don't look so good that you don't need practice," Coach bellowed.

The team ran through their plays, everyone avoiding getting too close to Molly.

After dinner and a hot bath, Molly sat at her desk to do homework. The family had eaten early so her parents could go to the hospital and visit Mr. Brewer, but they weren't quite ready to go yet.

Molly took a piece of blue construction paper and cut out a heart. She made little slits along the edges and laced a white ribbon through the slits, tying a bow at the top. Gluing a small gold heart in the center, she sat back and smiled at the results. GET WELL SOON, she printed in block letters.

"Dad, will you please give this to Mr. Brewer?" she asked as he put his coat on.

"Not more cookies, I hope?" her dad said, turning the envelope with the special heart in it over in his hands.

"No. It's a sort of September Valentine," Molly said, kissing him goodbye.

He returned the kiss, sniffing. "You don't smell like an onion factory anymore. Does Colleen know you used her bubble bath?"

"How did you know?" Molly's mouth fell open.

"Good nose. Better tell her," he added, going out the door.

"Better tell who what?" asked Colleen, coming in from play rehearsal and heading for the kitchen where her mother had kept her dinner warm.

"Better tell you I used your bubble bath. *Wait!* Don't get mad," Molly pleaded as Colleen whirled and her eyes squinted into furious slits.

She told Colleen the whole story, starting with the perfume in class and ending with the explanation she gave the boys about onions making them macho.

The corners of Colleen's mouth twitched, then she was laughing out loud.

"I don't know how those boys stand you," she said. "But you're not getting off scot-free for taking my bubble bath without permission. Now you can help me with the dishes. You clear." Colleen was still chuckling as she went into the kitchen.

Molly hated doing dishes. It was a big price to pay, but she had to pay it. She began scraping all the plates into the empty stew tureen.

Maybe I'll just make a magic potion, she thought. Into the big tureen she poured half a salt shaker, some pepper, all the left over milk, some strawberry jello that had liquefied, and gravy from the stew. It didn't look right. Carrying the empty plates into the kitchen, she got a bottle of vinegar and some baking soda from the pantry. She put half the box of baking soda into the tureen, then poured vinegar in until the whole mess began to bubble and froth.

Molly smiled. A perfect end to a crazy day.

Chapter Fourteen

The phone was ringing when Molly walked in from school.

"Hello?" she answered breathlessly.

"Well, Girl, you made my day. When your Dad gave me that Valentine last night I all but flooded the halls."

"Mr. Brewer! Are you in a regular room now?"

"You bet. And I'm getting so ornery they'll probably be sending me home soon, just to get rid of me. Yesiree, it won't be long."

"I'm so glad. You sound just like yourself."

"Who did you expect me to sound like? Grover?"

Molly laughed.

"I mean it about that card, Girl. When I saw it my eyes filled up and so did my heart. You do me more good than all the medicine they pour down me."

"I'm glad you liked it."

"Yes sir, only you would have thought of a Valentine made with the colors of the Fighting Irish of Notre Dame. It's the best Valentine I ever had."

"Will you be able to play football with me when you get home?"

"Not for a while yet. They tell me I'm an old man and I need plenty of rest. But I'll tell you what we *can* do."

"What?"

"We can bake cookies!"

Molly was surprised. "Can you bake cookies?" she asked.

"Sure I can. I make a mean batch of peanut butter chewies."

"Wow. It's hard to picture a man like you baking cookies."

"Why?"

"I don't know. I guess I think of mothers baking cookies, that's all."

"You listen here, Girl. Some of the very best cooks in the world are men. They call them *master chefs*."

"No kidding. Wow."

"After all, if girls can play football, men should be able to bake cookies," Mr. Brewer said slyly.

Molly laughed. "You've got me there," she said. Then added, "Why haven't you told Mom you do that stuff? She always thinks you're suffering all alone with no homemade goodies, so she bakes for you."

"I'm not stupid, Girl. Your mother is a wonderful cook. Now bugger off and let an old man get some rest."

Molly was still smiling when she hung up the phone.

"Wind sprints. On the double!" Coach yelled. Molly took off, loving the feel of the cool afternoon wind in her face. With her helmet, goggles, and face guard on she was always hot. The faster she ran, the better she felt. She was happy. No one questioned who she was on the team. Mr. Brewer was coming home soon. She'd gotten an A on her math test today. Colleen wasn't mad at her for a change. And her first football game was fast approaching.

"Line up for the meat grinder," Coach bellowed.

Molly fell in behind Bobby, running in place as she waited her turn at the grinder.

She watched as Jason took his turn. Just before he reached the two guys he was supposed to run between, he bent low. The two guys crashed into each other and Jason got through untouched. Molly was impressed. That was a piece of strategy she hadn't seen before.

Bobby took his turn and landed face down in the grass.

Molly got positioned in a three-point stand (both feet and one hand on the ground), then ran toward the grinder. Just as she got close enough to see their eyelashes, she dropped, ducked her head, and shot like a bullet between them.

Jason had been watching and clapped heartily. "All right! That was great."

"Thanks. But you should take the credit. You showed me how."

"That's what team play is all about, isn't it?" He was smiling and Molly felt something warm turn over inside. For weeks she had been concentrating so hard on hating Jason that she hadn't even noticed he could sometimes be almost human. Suddenly, in the bright autumn sunshine there on the football field, Molly realized she actually wished she didn't hate Jason so much.

But there wasn't any more time to think about it. Coach was so intent on going over plays and mastering everything before the game next week, there wasn't time for anything else. They practiced long and hard.

When Molly got home and into her bath, she was so exhausted she thought she'd fall asleep right there in the tub. But when her dad knocked on the bathroom door and told her dinner was ready, she jumped right out.

Wrapping her terry cloth bathrobe around herself, she hurriedly picked up her uniform, took it in her room, and dumped it on the floor.

As she combed her hair, Molly took a good look at the face staring back at her from the mirror.

Slowly, she put the comb down and said out loud, "You're a fraud. You're not even honest with yourself. No, don't turn away. Face it. You've hated Jason all along because he has such warped ideas about what girls should do. But what about *your* warped ideas? Why were you so

82

surprised when Mr. Brewer told you he bakes cookies? Because he's a *man*, that's why. And men aren't supposed to bake cookies, right? *Wrong!*"

Molly brought her face so close to the mirror her nose touched it, then she crossed her eyes.

"But that *still* doesn't excuse creep-o Jason!"

She stuck out her tongue and turned her back on the mirror, then ran down to dinner.

Chapter Fifteen

The phone was ringing but Molly didn't even look up from her homework. It was always for Colleen these days.

She was surprised when her mother called her.

"Molly, it's for you," she said, then whispered with her hand over the phone, "It's a boy!"

A boy? What boy would be calling her?

She picked up the phone and said "Hello."

She didn't hear anything at first, then a muffled giggle. Then someone recited in a sing-song voice:

> *"Molly is a frog*
> *Molly is a frog.*
> *I thought she was a red-haired dog*
> *But now I know she's just a frog!"*

More giggles, then the line went dead.

Jason! Who else? The jerk.

She went back to doing her homework.

A few minutes later, the phone rang again.

"It's for you, Molly," her mother said.

"I'm busy."

"Molly, you're wanted on the phone," her mother insisted.

"Tell him," she thought a minute. "Tell him I got bit by an African Zulu fly and I'm having convulsions, so I can't come to the phone right now."

"Molly, it's Arabella."

"Why didn't you say so?" she asked crossly, picking up the phone.

"What the heck's an African Zulu fly?" Arabella asked.

"Something I made up. For Jason."

"Jason?"

"Yeah. He called a few minutes ago with one of his stupid poems. Now I'm a frog."

"That jerk. Listen, I'm calling about the skating party tomorrow night. You're going, aren't you?"

"Sure. The Mastermind is planning to super glue my skate wheels. I wouldn't miss it for the world."

"When is he going to learn?" Arabella wondered. "Anyway," she continued, "my mom bought me the cutest new pink skating outfit. I wondered if you want to wear my blue one. You know, with the full skirt that twirls when you go around?"

"Thanks, but I'm wearing jeans. Easier on the knees."

"Molly, you know you never fall down. Why don't you wear something pretty?"

"I'd much rather be comfortable than pretty."

Arabella sighed. "If you change your mind . . ."

"I know. Thanks."

"Molly?" Arabella hesitated.

"Yeah?"

"If one of the boys asked you to skate with him, would you?"

"Are you kidding? I wouldn't be caught dead skating with any of those guys. I'd probably catch hoobie-goobie disease from their sweaty hands or something."

"Oh." Arabella's voice was so soft Molly barely heard it.

"Why?"

"I just wondered."

"Why?" Molly asked again.

"I kinda thought it might be fun to, you know, skate with Bobby. Just once, of course," Arabella was quick to add.

"Brother," Molly said under her breath. "I never thought I'd see the day when my best friend would get interested in dweebs."

The skating rink was noisy with the sound of a jillion kids and music playing too loud. The constant whir of skates was background to all the conversations and shouted greetings.

Molly couldn't help feeling excited as she and Arabella took their skates to a quiet corner to put on. They had turned in their shoes at the skate exchange and Molly wondered idlely how Jason planned to super glue her skate wheels together, when he suddenly appeared at her elbow.

"There's a call for you, Molly-O. Out at the desk."

"For me? Who is it?"

"How should I know? I was just told to get you."

Molly put her skates down and started across the carpeted floor toward the desk.

No way! she thought, turning and going back to where Jason had just picked up her skates.

Molly grabbed them away from him. "What are you doing?" she asked suspiciously.

"I was just holding them for you. They always go around picking up the skates that are lying around so they don't lose any. You know that."

"Yeah. I'll bet."

"Take them with you then, if you don't believe me."

"I don't," she said, grabbing the skates, but not before she noticed the tube of Super Glue sticking out of his pocket. She smiled as she headed for the desk.

"Is there a call for Molly Maguire?" she asked the bored-looking lady next to the telephone.

"No calls," was the curt reply.

I knew it, Molly thought. *The liar.*

She hurriedly put on her skates and looked around for Arabella.

It was hard to walk on the carpet with skates, so Molly headed for the rink.

She stood at the entrance for a minute, watching all the faces whirl past, and she spotted Arabella.

She was in the middle of the skating rink where all the good skaters were doing tricks. She looked so pretty in her new pink outfit skating backwards to the music.

Molly started skating toward the middle, but before she got there Bobby Stowe skated up to Arabella and started talking to her.

Molly watched as Arabella shyly put her hand in Bobby's and they started out together.

I don't believe this, Molly thought as she just coasted along, no longer moving her feet. Her eyes were trained on Bobby and Arabella, moving slowly ahead of her. Arabella looked down and giggled at something Bobby said. He was grinning from ear to ear. Arabella was blushing.

Molly was suddenly conscious of her jeans and sweatshirt. She looked down and saw the grass stains on her knees. She hadn't even bothered to put on clean jeans. When she was getting dressed it hadn't seemed important what she wore. But now she felt like a slob.

"Ribitt, ribitt, ribitt!"

The Kermit the Frog sound came up behind her and blasted in her ear as a flash of red whizzed by. Jason!

Unconsciously, Molly's legs began moving faster and faster until she had passed Arabella and Bobby and was right behind Jason.

She poured on the steam and hunched down

on her skates, cutting right in front of him in practically a sitting position.

Jason was so surprised when he looked down and saw Molly that he lost his balance. He went down with a thud and Molly looked over her shoulder to see him spread out on the rink, rubbing his elbow. She smiled smugly and skated off to the carpeted area. "Splat," she whispered.

A few minutes later she was sitting at a table having a Dr. Pepper. Arabella was still off with Bobby, and Molly didn't feel like skating alone.

Jason pulled the chair out across from her and sat down.

"That was mean," he said.

"And I suppose it wasn't mean to super glue my skate wheels together?"

"What? How did you . . . ?"

"I knew you wanted my skates for something, then I saw the Super Glue in your pocket."

He just said, "Well, I didn't do it, did I?"

But only because I took my skates with me to the desk, Molly thought.

"You know, you remind me of someone I play football with. You move just like him. Do you have a cousin or someone about our same age?"

Molly almost spilled her drink. Her mouth opened wide.

"Nope," she said, closing it tight.

"He has freckles just like you, too," Jason said.

"Who is he?" Molly asked, stalling.

"Name's Lee Brewer. He goes to St. Raphael's. Know him?"

"Nope," she said again. Then she *had* to ask, "Is he good?"

"Yeah, real good. All the guys like him. He's fast and he never hogs the ball. He's a great wide receiver."

"Oh." It was taking all Molly's self-control to keep from smiling.

"It's funny," Jason continued. "None of us ever see him around town or anywhere. I mean, he's gotta hang out *someplace,* but we never see him except at practice."

"Maybe he turns into a werewolf after dark," Molly offered.

"You're so dumb," Jason said, standing. "I should have known better than to talk to you."

Molly was still biting the insides of her cheeks to keep from laughing when Arabella sat down in a rush, all out of breath.

"Guess what?" she asked and continued without waiting for an answer. "Bobby asked me to skate and we skated to *four* records! Isn't that great?"

Molly didn't particularly think so, but she smiled and said, "Um hum."

"And you know what else? Bobby told me about 'Lee'. He thinks you're a terrific player. What's going to happen when they find out?"

"I don't know. But they better not find out. Criminey, if they knew I was 'Lee', well, it would just destroy everything."

Molly watched the skaters. She saw Jason and Bobby going around together.

She'd really have to start being more careful.

Jason was already curious about Lee. Man, if they found out . . .

The next week seemed to fly by. Each day blended into the next as Molly practiced football, welcomed Mr. Brewer home, and tried to keep up with her homework. She and Colleen seemed to be getting along exceptionally well. When Colleen was home she was very agreeable and easy to please. She had that dreamy look on her face most of the time now and spent a good part of every day talking to Mike on the phone. Molly didn't understand it but she didn't question it, either. She was just glad Colleen didn't jump all over her for every little thing the way she used to.

Mr. Brewer was kind of weak, but he was back to being his old self. He sat on his front porch and talked her through different football plays. He still couldn't throw or catch, but he taught her lots of little tricks just the same.

At one point, he got serious and said, "Maybe we were wrong, Girl. Maybe it was wrong of me to encourage you to try to deceive the boys. It sounded like fun at the time, but maybe you should stop the masquerade before it gets any worse."

"No way. It's too late now," Molly said. "I can't tell them it's me. I *won't* tell them it's me." And she dropped the conversation right there.

The night before the first game, Molly moved restlessly around her room. She lay on her stomach on her bed, then jumped up and started rearranging the clutter on her dresser. She stacked her three library books on the floor, picked up the dirty socks they had been next to, tossed the socks on the closet floor, then plopped on her bed again.

Colleen sat watching her in disbelief. "What is *wrong* with you?" she asked.

"I don't know. I just feel all jiggly inside."

"Here, paint your fingernails," Colleen said, tossing her a bottle of bright red polish. "That always calms me down."

Molly looked at her nails. They were half bitten off and very jagged. "Thanks, but I can't wear this. The game tomorrow, remember?"

"Then paint your toenails. No one will ever see them."

"Okay." Molly pulled off her shoes and socks, picked the lint from between her toes, then began painting. Her hand was steady but she still managed to get red polish on her toes as well as her toenails. It didn't matter. No one would see it. And it did help to calm her down. She just couldn't wait for the game tomorrow. But she was also scared stiff. She almost wished the first game was already over with so the jillions of butterflies in her stomach would take off and leave her alone. By this time tomorrow it *would* be over with.

Molly sighed and put the nail polish away.

Chapter Sixteen

Saturday, September 23. Molly would never forget that day as long as she lived. The day of her very first football game.

She woke up at six A.M., unable to sleep another wink. Her stomach was doing summersaults as she lay in bed thinking of the game. What if she couldn't run fast? What if she forgot the plays? What if she fumbled every ball? What if she couldn't catch it or throw it? What if . . . what if . . . ? The one thing Molly didn't worry about was getting hurt. She had learned the hard way how to relax and fall like a rag doll. With all the pads in her uniform she never got hurt, no matter how rough the practice was.

It seemed to take forever for the rest of the family to get up, but they finally did. Her mom made Molly oatmeal, as usual, and her dad insisted she eat it. "You need something that will stick to your ribs, Pumpkin," he said. "You can't go out there and play football on an empty stomach."

She knew he was right, so she ate every bite. Besides, Molly really liked oatmeal. She didn't understand why so many kids thought it was yucky.

". . . and we'll be there by the time the game starts," her dad was saying.

"What?"

"We'll get Mr. Brewer and drive over to the park. We'll have to bring a chair for him and we'll use the car since he can't walk that far yet, but we'll be there in time for the game, don't worry."

"Worry? The game? Dad, *you can't* go to the game."

"What do you mean, I can't go?" her father exploded.

"It's just that, well, it's like practice, remember? If the guys see you at the game they'll wonder why you're there all of a sudden and then they'll know it's me, you know?"

"No, I *don't* know. Your mother and I will pick up Mr. Brewer and we *will* be at the game." Her dad's face was turning red.

Here it comes, Molly thought. *Lecture number 398 on the importance of parental support and don't deny us the right everyone else has of seeing our own daughter play football.*

"Okay. I'm sorry. But please don't yell my

name out loud." *And please, God, don't let the guys notice them,* she added silently.

By game time, Molly had put every thought and worry from her head. She was so excited she could hardly stand it. Bobby nudged her just before the first play.

"See that number 34 over there?"

"Yeah?"

"That's Dozer."

Molly swallowed hard. Number 34 was huge. His arms had ripples in them like a Sumo wrestler and his legs looked like tree trunks. He stood with his hands on his hips, glaring at them. Molly swallowed again.

It was obvious in the first three plays that Dozer would break every rule in the book, but only when he could do it without getting caught. He tackled Ray and when he had him down on the ground, he stuck his finger in Ray's eye. Ray yelped, but Dozer just got up and brushed himself off, walking away with a smile on his face.

In another play there was a dog pile, three guys from each team down with Dozer on top. He bit the back of Bobby's leg.

Molly saw all this and couldn't believe it.

The next time she was close to Dozer, she hissed, "What's the matter with you? We want to play football, not fight. Why do you have to be such a bully?"

He grinned. "You're next, Babyface!"

A few minutes later, Bobby threw a long pass to her and she was running to catch it when she saw Dozer out of the corner of her eye, heading right for her. Something flashed between them, and she caught the ball and ran like the wind for the goal line. Touchdown!

When she looked back she saw Dozer rolling on the ground with . . . Jason! *He* had been the flash and had permitted her to score. Dozer stood up and planted his cleats squarely on Jason's foot in a grinding motion, then walked away. No one but Molly saw it. And now she saw the fire in Jason's eyes. He came up behind Dozer and grabbed his face mask, swinging him around.

Whistles blew, referees waved their arms, and Coach yelled.

When they were all huddled together, Coach said, "What did I tell you guys about fighting? You just cost us fifteen yards, Jenson. You certainly did not display good sportsmanship back there. Now if you want to play on my team, you play by the rules. Understand?"

"But Coach," Bobby began.

"Don't 'But Coach' me. I don't care what the reasons are, there will be *no fighting* on my team!"

Back in the game, Dozer openly snickered. "What's a matter, Nambie Pambies? Papa want you to be good little boys? Goodie goodies!"

The rest of the first half went progressively downhill. Molly felt totally defeated. They all did. They hadn't been able to score again, and the Lancers had made three touchdowns. The score was 18–6.

Walking off the field, Ray said, "Hey Guys! I

got a great idea! I still have a couple of onions in my bag. Let's go get them and smear ourselves with them. We'll out-stink the Lancers if nothing else, and it may just give us the macho power we need."

"Super!"

"Let's go!"

"All right!"

Molly rolled her eyes but didn't say anything. She wasn't about to tell them the onions were worthless.

In the third quarter the Lancers avoided contact with them whenever possible. Molly and the boys acted as though everything was normal, but the onion odor was so overpowering she was getting nauseated. It was obviously affecting the Lancers, too, and Molly could see Dozer getting madder by the minute.

That made her feel better.

She dropped back to catch a pass and turned, heading for the goal line. Dozer was coming at her like a truck at full speed. For a minute Molly's knees turned to Jello, then she poured the steam on and ran for all she was worth. The goal line was getting closer, but so was Dozer. Faster and faster she ran, and faster and faster came Dozer. She heard the thump of his cleats in the grass, the ragged breathing through his mouthpiece as he got closer. One yard from the goal line, Molly took a dive with the ball out in front of her. She cleared the line and made a touchdown!

But in the next second she felt a searing,

wrenching pain as her leg crunched under Dozer's full weight.

When she opened her eyes through a red haze, Molly looked up into Coach's face, with the referees and Jason and Bobby and Ray and the other guys all around her.

Coach was gently touching her leg, feeling the bones, when she screamed. It hurt so bad she couldn't stand it.

"I'm sorry, Lee. I won't touch it again. Let me take off your cleats in case there's swelling," Coach said, taking off her shoe and sock and exposing her bright red toenails.

The faces around her all looked shocked, then curious. Jason reached over and unstrapped her helmet, slipping it off her head. He pulled off the white cotton cap and her long red hair cascaded out over the grass.

Chapter Seventeen

Sunday, September 24. The day after the best/ worst day of Molly's life.

Her dad carried her downstairs and put her on the couch with three pillows under her broken leg. The doctor in the emergency room had put a nice, light fiberglass cast on it yesterday, but it still hurt and she still couldn't do anything by herself. Not even go to the bathroom. Her mother put a little bell on the coffee table so Molly could call for help when she needed to go.

Molly felt dismal. Her secret was out. Everyone knew about her playing football now. Even Miss Bloom had called last night to see how she was doing.

Arabella came over right after Molly got home from the hospital yesterday. She brought Molly a funny book by Beverly Cleary about a mouse. Molly knew she'd have plenty of time to read it.

Arabella also brought her a pack of felt tip markers. "For people to write on your cast," she said. That was a good idea. Arabella was the first to write something. She wrote:

> *Roses are red*
> *Violets are blue*
> *Your foot's gonna stink*
> *Without a shoe.*

That didn't really help matters a whole lot.

Colleen saw the markers and said, "Let me use the red one, Mol. For something special."

"Nope. No one gets the red one. Pick any other color you want."

"Why not red?"

"It's special. I'm saving it."

"Oh, all right." Colleen picked purple. She made a big purple heart and wrote C.M. + M.D. in the middle.

"It's *my* leg, not his," Molly complained.

Colleen took the purple marker again and wrote:

Get well soon. The dishes will be waiting.

Molly read it and shook her head. Nothing was making her feel any better.

Just before dinner, Ray and Bobby came over. They gave Molly a big, fat Hershey bar. They told her they really missed her in the rest of the game. They told her all about how the Lancers won 18–12, but that she should really feel good because she made the twelve points for their team.

"And guess what?" Bobby said. "Dozer got kicked out! Can you believe it? He finally got caught. *Everybody* saw what he did to you, and when the refs found out you were a girl, they *really* gave it to him! He won't play any more this year," Bobby said, looking at Molly's cast. "Course, you won't either, I guess," he finished quietly.

"Yeah, I know." Molly picked at the cast, holding back her tears.

"You really surprised us, Molly," Ray said shyly. "You're a terrific football player."

"Thanks." That helped.

"All the guys thought you did a good job. All except Jason. He won't talk about it," Ray added.

"Guess he's pretty mad at me, huh?"

"He's madder than a hornet. He says that was a rotten thing for a dumb girl to do," Bobby answered. "No offense, Molly. I'm just telling you what he said."

"I know. It's okay."

While Molly lay on the couch remembering, the doorbell rang. It was Mr. Brewer.

"Should you be out?" she asked.

"Sure I should. I'm in better shape than you are, Girl."

"I guess so."

"Besides, I told your folks I'd come over and

stay with you while they go to church. You're not going this Sunday, Twinkle Toes!"

Molly tried to rearrange herself and felt a sharp stab of pain.

"You just stay put, Girl. Then it won't hurt. I've got something here to make you feel better, I think."

He reached in his coat pocket and pulled out a video tape, then gave it to her.

Molly slid the cassette out of its cardboard case and read, *Notre Dame vs. USC, 1988*.

"Ohhh," she sighed. "I remember you telling me about this game. Notre Dame won 27–10, right?"

"Yup, that's right. Want to watch it?"

"Please. Put it on."

Molly got herself comfortable as the football game started. It was a great game, but the more she watched it, the more depressed she got. She wondered if she'd ever be able to play football again. Would her leg heal? Would she be able to run fast? Or was it all over?

She looked at her leg in the cast and felt the tears running down her cheeks.

She was dozing on the couch later that afternoon when the doorbell rang again. Molly didn't pay any attention. She felt too depressed to care who was visiting.

"Hi."

Her eyes flew open and she looked squarely at Jason.

"What are you doing here? I mean, I thought

you hated me," Molly said, so surprised to see him she stuttered.

"I do. I did." Jason was a little uncomfortable, too. "What I mean is, I think it was a pretty dirty trick you pulled, but . . ."

"But what?"

"Well, I have to admit you're tough. I never would have thought you could play so well. You really have guts, Molly."

Was she hearing right? Was Jason admitting she, a *girl,* could play football as well as the boys?

"Thanks." Her voice was so small she could hardly hear it herself. Somehow, the taste of victory was not very sweet.

"I'm sorry," she said, her voice clear now.

"About what?"

"That *was* a dirty trick. I wish we could start all over. I mean, I still want to play football, but I wish I had played as myself instead of trying to be someone else."

"Why did you do it?" he asked.

"To prove to the boys, to *you,* that a girl doesn't have to stay home and play with dolls all the time. Girls like to do the same things boys do. I happen to love football, but there's no way you could ever understand that."

Jason sat there looking at the floor for a long time. "You know," he said. "My mom thinks you're terrific." He smiled and added, "But not my dad!"

Molly had to smile, too. Some things never changed.

"Is that a movie?" Jason asked, noticing the video cassette on the table.

"It's the ND-USC game from 1988."

"You're kidding," he said, his eyes huge. "Man, I'd love to see that game. Can I watch it with you?"

"Sure. Put it on."

Before he did, he looked at Molly and said, "You know, for a girl, you're not bad."

"Thanks." That was quite a compliment from Jason.

"Want me to write on your cast?"

"Okay," Molly answered, handing him the red marker she had been saving. A slow smile spread across her face as she read the upside down letters:

TO THE GIRL WHO PLAYS
WIDE RECEIVER LIKE ONE OF THE GUYS.

It had all been worth it.

From Out of the Shadows...
Stories Filled With Mystery and Suspense by
MARY DOWNING HAHN

THE TIME OF THE WITCH
71116-8/$2.99 US/$3.50 Can
It is the middle of the night and suddenly Laura is awake, trembling with fear. Just beneath her bedroom window, a strange-looking old woman is standing in the moonlight. A big black crow is perched on her shoulder and she is looking up—staring back at Laura.

THE DEAD MAN IN INDIAN CREEK
71362-4/$3.50 US/$4.25 Can

THE DOLL IN THE GARDEN
70865-5/$3.50 US/$4.25 Can

FOLLOWING THE MYSTERY MAN
70677-6/$3.50 US/$4.25 Can

TALLAHASSEE HIGGINS
70500-1/$3.50 US/$4.25 Can

WAIT TILL HELEN COMES
70442-0/$3.50 US/$4.25 Can